G.G. Snowboards

By
Marty Mokler Banks

Photo Illustrations By
Alisa Mokler Harper

SWITCH MONKEY PRESS

SWITCH MONKEY PRESS, LLC
Colorado Springs, Colorado

CONTENTS

Chapter 1

The popcorn piece flew high above my face. I had to twist my neck and open my mouth really big, but... I caught it!

"Six," I said as I chewed. This was a new record.

My dog, Pretzel, stared at me.

See, we have this game. I sit upside down on the couch, with my feet up high and my head hanging down. I like to watch TV this way. It makes all the shows better.

Then I get a bowl of popcorn and hold it on my stomach. I toss one piece of popcorn and try to catch it in my mouth. I like to see

how many I can catch in a row. If I miss,
Pretzel gets to eat it.

Pretzel *loves* this game.

Hanging out, watching TV. . . upside down.

As I was about to attempt seven in a
row, Dad came home early from work.

"Hey, G.G.," he said. "How's spring break
so far?"

"Pretty good. I'm trying to get to twenty in a row."

"Ah," he said. "Impressive."

"Yep."

"Maybe I have a better plan," he said. "We can go to the mountains."

I tossed a popcorn piece. Aw, dang it, I missed. "Okay," I said.

My family goes to the Rocky Mountains a lot. My Aunt Christina and Uncle Frank live there, near a ski area. We usually build a snowman and stuff like that. It's okay.

But what I really want to do is learn to snowboard. Every time I ask, though, my mom says it costs too much. Or it's summer and there's no snow. My cousin, Carlos, got to learn two years ago. *So* not fair.

I love to build snowmen, but I'd rather snowboard. True fact.

So going to the mountains does not get me too excited.

I tossed another popcorn piece. Dang it, missed again.

Dad said, "Also, I have a surprise."

My hand stopped in the popcorn bowl. "Yeah?"

"Yeah," he said. "This time I thought we could snowboard."

I rolled my feet over my head and stood up as popcorn flew all over the room.

"SNOWBOARD?" I asked. "Really? Really, really?"

"Really, really," said Dad. "We'll go up later today—when Mom, Grandma and Bell come back from the store."

"Can Pretzel come?"

"I think it would be better if he stayed with Isaac. Why don't you go ask if it's okay?"

I ran down the stairs to Isaac's. He lives one floor below us, in our apartment building in Denver. He's also in my class. I don't care that he's a boy—he's still a good friend.

When Isaac opened his door, I jumped up and down and yelled, "I get to learn to SNOWBOARD!"

He covered his ears. "Ouch."

"Sorry," I said.

He uncovered his ears. "When?"

"We leave later today."

He asked, "Do I get to keep Pretzel?"

"If your dad says okay."

We found Isaac's dad working on his laptop. He likes Pretzel, so he didn't even look up when he said, "Sure. All week?"

"Yep," I said. "I get to learn to snowboard."

"That's nice," he said. I don't think he really listened, but that's okay.

I told Isaac I'd be back later, with Pretzel and his food. "But maybe don't feed him a ton today. He's already had lots of popcorn."

"You missed?" Isaac asked. He knows about my game.

"Kind of."

"Okay," Isaac said. "Bye, Geeg."

Isaac is the only one who calls me "Geeg." Everybody else calls me G.G. Except when I'm in trouble. Then I hear very loudly, *Gabriela Garcia!*

I hear my whole big name *a lot.*

Anyway, I left Isaac's and went to the elevator. I use the elevator when I'm not in a hurry. I love to push those buttons.

When the door opened, Mom, Grandma Garcia and my sister, Bell, were inside.

"Hey, guess what?" I said, getting in with them. "We're going to the mountains to snowboard!"

"Aw," Bell wailed, "Mom! You said I got to tell G.G.!"

Then Bell stuck out her bottom lip. That is what Bell does when she doesn't get her way. In our family, we call it The Lip. And it usually lasts all day.

Little sisters are a PAIN.

But today it didn't even bother me. Today I was going to the mountains. To snowboard.

And not even a little sister could ruin that!

Chapter 2

It was not my fault The Lip came out—
again—in the car.

When we left our apartment, Dad said
we'd be at my aunt and uncle's house in no
time. To me, that meant super quick.

Super quick went by and we were still in
the city. So I asked nicely, "When will we get
there?"

"Soon, G.G.," said Dad. "Be patient."

Every kid knows that soon means
FOREVER. Frustrating!

The second time I asked when we would
get there, Mom said, "Didn't you bring your
Eye Spy game?"

Yes, I did bring my Eye Spy game.

But I was bored with Eye Spy way back at super quick. I'd put it down and Bell picked it up. She'd had it the whole time.

So I took it back.

Driving in the car on a long trip is soooo boring!

Now don't you think it's unfair that Bell kicked the back of Dad's seat, screamed *and* put out The Lip... and I got in trouble?

I do.

I crossed my MAD arms.

Meanwhile, Bell yelled and lipped, Dad sighed and Grandma Garcia hummed to block out the noise.

It was loud in that car.

Mom tried to change the mood. She said, "Aren't you two excited to learn to snowboard? What do you think you'll do first?"

Bell roared, "I DON'T KNOOOOOOOOW!"

Well. I knew.

I played snowboard Wii at Isaac's a lot. AND I'd seen snowboarders on TV. That was so cool I even watched it sitting right side up. So I knew *all* about it.

"First," I told my family, "I'm going to the terrain park and ride some rails. Then I'll catch some big air on a few jumps. Then I'll ride the halfpipe."

Not only did this make everyone in the car go quiet, but The Lip went away, too.

"Um," Dad said finally, "that's very bold, G.G. But maybe you could start smaller. Like with a ride on the lift."

Ha! I thought my family knew me better than that.

"Nope, Dad. I'm going to shred all week."

"What's shred?" asked Bell.

I said, "It's when snowboarders go down the hill."

I'd seen snowboarders on TV in the X Games and the Olympics. That was so exciting, I even watched that stuff right side up!

"Oh," she said. "Is it hard?"

"Nope," I said. "Well, maybe."

"Why don't we just see how it goes," said Mom.

"Yeah," said Dad. "Let's not make any big plans for now."

Well. I wasn't going to finally get to snowboard and just wait and see.

Nope.

So I said, "It's the halfpipe or nothing, Dad. And that's final."

Chapter 3

The next morning, Aunt Christina made pancakes and bacon because a good breakfast is very important. That's what Mom always says when I make a face at runny eggs.

Which are GROSS.

But eating with cousins is a different kind of problem.

"Carlos," I said, "you got syrup on my pants!"

"So?" Then he stuck out his tongue. Carlos is nine—only one year older than me. But sometimes he still acts like he's in kindergarten. He's a hard cousin to have.

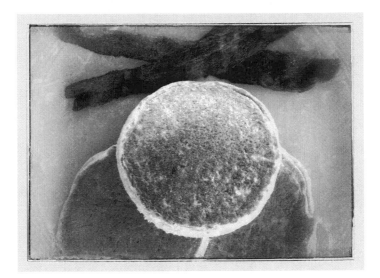

Bacon and pancakes—yummo!

I ignored him. Today was too special to let Carlos bug me.

I asked, "May I have more orange juice, please?"

"Sorry, kiddo, all gone," said Uncle Frank. "Who wants the last pancake?"

"Me-me-meeeeeeee," said my other cousin, Cari. She is little like Bell so she is sometimes a pain.

Still, I was not going to get grumpy.

"All right everybody," said Uncle Frank. "Go get ready. We leave in half an hour."

I jumped up from the table and ran to my big bag of stuff. I had to put it all on because it's very cold on the mountain. I saw it on the Discovery Channel (upside down).

First, if your hands and feet get too cold, you get frostbite. That's not when a big snow monster bites you, it's when your fingers and toes get so cold they fall off. Actually, first they turn black and THEN they fall off. Gross.

Also, you have to wear goggles over your eyes or you might get snow blind. That's when the snow gets so bright it pokes light icicles deep into your eyes and you can never see again. *Ever.*

Also, you have to wear a helmet. Everyone knows why. Duh.

Here is what I put on, very carefully, so I wouldn't get poked by light or have fingers fall off:

1.   Extra thick socks. I like my toes and want to keep them.

2.   Stretchy pants. Mom calls them yoga pants, but I don't do yoga. I just wear the pants.

3.   A shirt that comes up to your chin. It's called a turtleneck because it makes you look like a turtle in a shell. Weird.

Goggles? Check. Mittens? Check. Warm Socks? Check.
Helmet? Duh. Time to snowboard!

4.   Snow pants. They keep you from getting wet. Very important. Because if you get wet, you get cold. If you get cold. . . there go body parts, falling off like crazy.

5. Jacket. Duh.

6. Helmet. Ditto duh.

7. Gloves. And not just any old mittens. These are extra special warm and thick so your fingers DO NOT FALL OFF.

8. Goggles. We already talked about those.

Once all my special mountain stuff was on, I went to the mudroom—where there was no mud, by the way. Weird!

The mud room was where we put all the snowboards and boots we'd rented the night before.

My snowboard went to my chin. Dad got one that goes to the top of his head because he likes to go fast, and a bigger snowboard goes faster. Dad's snowboard is HUGE.

I put on my boots, picked up my snowboard and went out to Uncle Frank's van. I was ready!

But my family was slooooow.

So I waited.

And waited.

And waited.

Finally, Bell, Carlos, Cari, Dad, Mom and Uncle Frank were ready to go. Aunt Christina and Grandma Garcia were going to stay home and watch a movie. Boring!

I put my snowboard in the back of the van and buckled in my seatbelt.

I was so excited I had to wiggle my legs just a little, but I did not kick the back of Uncle Frank's seat. No I did not. This was a special day, and I was screaming so loud inside that I had to be very quiet outside.

Uncle Frank started the van.

Halfpipe—here I come!

Belted in and ready to go snowboarding!

Chapter 4

At the ski mountain, we were in a big, crowded parking lot. Lots of people must have had Dad's good idea to go to the mountains this week because we had to park far, far away from the slope.

I picked up my snowboard and started walking.

For a minute it was easy.

Then it got HARD.

First of all, my big snowboard boots felt like ginormous blocks on my feet. And the board was long and heavy, with sharp metal edges.

By the time we got to the slope I was EXHAUSTED. My arms and legs were so tired they wanted to fall off. But, they didn't.

At the ski slope, Carlos said, "The lift is over here."

Now, I know on the car ride up to the mountains I didn't think anything about the lift. But I'd never seen one up close.

Have you ever seen a lift? It's this flying metal couch that whizzes up behind you and whisks you into the air. People have no time to get comfy or anything because the chair is moving the whole time. If you miss or slide off or get sideways. . . CRASH.

So I said, "Um. . . ."

Dad said, "Don't worry, G.G. Uncle Frank is going to show you, Bell and Cari how to snowboard down here, first."

The lift is pretty much like a flying couch.

I DO NOT try to sit upside down on this couch!

"Not on the lift?"

"No. Everybody starts on the bunny slope first, where it's a little easier. Maybe you can go up on the lift later."

Now, I will tell you I was RELIEVED. But I couldn't really admit that.

So I said, "Awwww! Why does Carlos get to go and I don't?"

Carlos, of course, stuck out his tongue. See what I mean?

"Since Carlos already knows how to snowboard," said Dad, "he'll go with me and Mom for awhile."

Mom said, "After lunch we'll all go up on the lift. Together."

I still had to act a little upset. For one thing, Cari and Bell were littler than me. So I dragged my feet. It wasn't all that much of an act because those dogs were tired. Did you know people call feet "dogs?" Weird! But also kind of funny.

"Ruff. Ruff-ruff," said my feet.

So even though I acted a little sad, inside I was happy that I was with Uncle Frank.

Snowboarding is exciting. And maybe, for the first time, just a teeny, tiny, eenie, weenie bit scary.

My dogs were barking in those snowboard boots!

Chapter 5

The bunny slope was first of all, A Hill.

I am a strong girl. And I like to move. So any other day, I would run up the hill as fast as the wind.

But did I tell you that I was kind of tired? Those boots and snowboard were getting so, so, so heavy!

So although I hate it when other kids whine, I kind of whined, "Uncle Frank, do we have to climb that hill?"

"What?" asked Uncle Frank with a big surprise face. "You don't want to carry that snowboard all day?"

I like Uncle Frank.

"Nope!" I said.

"Okay then," he said. "Let's take the magic carpet to the top."

The... magic carpet?

Uncle Frank walked over to a long piece of rubber that looked like a big, skinny rug. It went from the bottom of the hill to the top. When we got next to it, I saw that it moved.

Ah ha! Now I understood magic carpet.

"Now," he said, "you know how the mall has escalators?"

"Stairs that move!" I said. I love things that move.

"That's it," said Uncle Frank. "Well, this magic carpet is just like that. You step onto it and hold still. It will take you to the top. Then you step off."

You don't even have to be Aladdin to ride this magic carpet.

"I'm scared," said Cari.

"Me, too," said Bell.

"Not me!" I said. This looked awesome.

"Okay then, kiddo," said Uncle Frank.
"You first."

I held my snowboard with one arm.
Then I got my balance. I took one step.
Whoa! Wobble. I had to use my free arm to
balance and quick put my other foot on the

magic carpet. It started to take me up the hill.

At first I kind of bobbled around, like those heads you see in the back windows of cars. But then I was all in balance again.

"Woo hoo!" I yelled. "I'm going up!"

Chapter 6

We all made it to the top of the bunny slope, and nobody fell off the magic carpet.

"Now, ladies," said Uncle Frank, "everybody put down your snowboard. Wait, Bell, where it's flat!" Then he ran after Bell's snowboard because it got excited and started down the hill without her.

Once all of our snowboards were flat on the snow, Uncle Frank said, "First we learn to strap in. Everybody put your front foot on your board, inside the big straps."

Now right away, we got confused. That's because Uncle Frank said Bell and I ride regular, but Cari rides goofy.

A regular rider is somebody who stands on his board with his left foot in front. Like if he were pointed downhill, the left foot would be the one to reach the bottom first.

I don't know what's so regular about that!

But a goofy rider stands on his board with his right foot in front. I don't think a right foot is very goofy, but I do know Cari is a goofy girl, so it all made sense to me.

Also, it wasn't a surprise when Uncle Frank said, "Oops, Cari, turn around. You're backwards."

Finally we got our front feet and back feet straight and in the big straps.

I pulled the strap tight over one foot and then the other. Woo hoo! I was connected to my snowboard.

Strapped in and ready to go!

Uncle Frank asked, "Now ladies, do you know how to squat?"

So while I went into the best squat ever, Uncle Frank showed Cari and Bell that a squat is just a pretend sit. "Bend your knees," he told them many, many, *many* times.

That is the problem with learning something with little kids. All the directions are too easy.

"Now everybody put your hands out in front of you," he said. "No, Cari, not over your head. In front of you. Good."

My hands were perfectly in front of me, of course.

"Now point your shoulder in the direction you want to go. No, don't point at a tree, Bell. Bad idea."

I was not pointing my shoulder at a tree. No I was not. I was pointing to the biggest, widest place I could see.

"All right, ladies," said Uncle Frank. "Moment of truth. We do all three things at once. And then we shred down the hill."

"No!" screamed Cari.

If Uncle Frank could have seen inside my goggles, he would have seen me roll my eyes.

Or maybe he did.

"G.G.," he said. "Why don't you go first?"

I squatted. The best squat ever!

I put my hands out in front of me. Hands in the perfect spot!

And I pointed my shoulder toward the bottom of the hill. . . .

Chapter 7

"I'm shredding!"

As soon as my shoulder turned the right way, my perfect squat and hands in front of me made the board move forward.

"Look where you want to go," yelled Uncle Frank.

Well. I did not look at that tree.

No I did not.

I zoomed to the bottom of the hill as the wind hit my face. Inside my helmet a funny whistle noise blew and my toes tingled with excitement.

Shred monster on the move.

The whole time I looked toward a big open space. And then it was flat and I stopped.

IT WAS AWESOME!

I looked up to the top of the hill and Uncle Frank was giving me two big thumbs up. I was very happy.

Happy, happy, happy.

Until I had to wait, wait, wait for those two little girls to come down the hill. Which took FOREVER.

Bell finally got going on her own, but she waved her hands around and fell—plop—right on her butt.

Then Cari was boarding down the hill.

"Yeah, Cari!" I yelled.

Cari was starting to go really fast. But her shoulder was pointed right at Bell, still on her butt in the snow.

Uncle Frank started running after Cari. "Turn your shoulders. Look to the side! WATCH OUT!"

Plop! Bell sprayed snow everywhere.

Well. You know what happened.

One big pile of little girls.

Uncle Frank finally got them untangled and going down the hill again.

"I'm shredding!" screamed Cari.

"Me, too!" yelled Bell.

I might even have clapped a little bit. Have you ever clapped with super special gloves on? It doesn't sound like hands. It sounds like the dryer when it gets stuck. Cla-clunk. Cla-clunk. That happens a lot in our apartment.

Anyway, when the girls were finally at the bottom of the hill, before I could even say it, Cari yelled, "Again!"

Little girl, shredding the bunny hill. Oh, ya.

We did the magic carpet and went down the hill four more times.

I decided this really wasn't so hard.

But then Uncle Frank said, "You're doing great, G.G. Now you need to learn how to turn."

Uh oh.

Chapter 8

Luckily, Bell and Cari were getting cranky. That is what happens when little kids get tired.

So Uncle Frank had a good idea. "How about a break."

"And hot chocolate?" I asked. That's me being helpful, by the way. I knew the little girls really wanted hot chocolate.

"Yeah!" Cari and Bell said.

"Okay," he said. "Hot chocolate."

We all undid our straps. We were now experts at that. Then we put our boards up against a big porch at the base lodge. That's the place where they sell hot chocolate.

*We had become total experts at strapping in
and out of our snowboards.*

Cari, Bell and I sat at a big picnic table outside. Uncle Frank went inside to get four hot chocolates with marshmallows swimming on top.

Did you know that hot chocolate is best when you've been outside in the snow shredding on the mountain?

True fact.

As I sipped my yummy hot chocolate and tried to get a little bit of melted marshmallow in each sip, Uncle Frank pointed to my hands.

"You can take off your gloves now, G.G."

"But I don't want to get frostbite and have my hands turn black and fall off," I said.

Uncle Frank gave me a confused look. And then he laughed. "It's okay to take them off for a little while. When we take our breaks."

I wasn't so sure about that.

"And you can take off your goggles, too," he said.

"But I don't want my eyes poked by light so strong I never see again. *Ever.*"

"I promise that won't happen. Just take them off while we stop," he said. "You can even take off your helmet. I don't think you'll fall off the bench."

Ha ha. Uncle Frank could be soooooo funny.

Well. I did not want to get frostbite and I did not want to get light poked.

But Uncle Frank still had his fingers. And he could still see. And he had his gloves and goggles and helmet off.

So I tried just for a minute.

HA!

It is much easier to drink hot chocolate when you have fingers to use.

"Okay," said Uncle Frank. "So here's the plan. We teach you how to turn. Then we stop for lunch. After that, G.G., I think you'll be ready to go up the lift with your mom and dad."

I choked on my hot chocolate. "*The Lift?*"

HOT CHOCOLATE! Sooo delicious.

"You'll be ready," he said.

Suddenly this shredding business didn't seem quite so easy.

Chapter 9

Uncle Frank was a good teacher. At least, he made it *sound* easy.

"To make a front-side turn, push with your toes so the front edge of your board digs in uphill, into the slope," he said. "And on the back-side turn, push in the back edge with your heels."

As I went down the bunny slope, I tried a front-side turn.

THUD.

"That's okay, G.G.," he said. "Stand up and try again.

So I did.

Thud.

But before that *thud*, I felt the board turn just a teeny, tiny bit.

"Better!" he said.

So I tried again.

And again.

And again.

Most of the time I hit the ground a lot. Sometimes really hard. But I felt the board turn a little better each time.

Meanwhile, Cari and Bell just kept going up the magic carpet, and then straight down the slope. They passed me like a zillion times.

By lunch, I had turned a lot. I was even getting kind of good at the front-side turns. But the back-side turns were hard. So here's what I did, all the way down the slope:

Front side: turn on a big curve!

Back side: dig in on the snowboard edge and Thud. Bounce! PLOP.

Front side: turn on a big curve!

Back side: dig in on the snowboard edge and Thud. Bounce! PLOP.

But that's okay. I sort of planned all those thuds and plops.

Okay, not really. But it was still fun.

True fact.

Falling down just means you get back up.
Again. . . and again.

While we ate lunch, I even took off my gloves, goggles and helmet.

And I didn't even lose body parts or eyesight. Phew!

But I knew even harder stuff was coming soon. . . .

Chapter 10

After lunch, the little girls said they wanted to watch movies with Aunt Christina and Grandma Garcia. So Uncle Frank took them home.

"Ready for the chair lift?" asked Dad.

"That's no chair," I said. "That's a couch!"

And they all laughed. Which was fine. Because while they laughed, I could be scared and nobody noticed.

Because I was about to go on *The Lift*.

The first thing you have to know is that getting on the lift is very COMPLICATED. Especially for a snowboarder.

People on skis get to just glide forward.

La la la. . . there go skiers, gliding forward, no problem.

But us snowboarders have to work hard. Our front foot is strapped in. But our back foot is free. We have to use our back foot to push the whole board forward, like on a skateboard.

Sounds easy, right?

Wrong!

Your front foot doesn't move AT ALL. So the rest of you bends and squiggles around while your back foot pushes. It's super exhausting.

But, I did it.

Next you get in line with lots of people. It's like being in the ball pit at Chuck E. Cheese. Everybody bumps into each other as they move forward. And the skiers have poles with spikes on the end.

It's amazing I lived through it.

When you finally get to the front of the line, the lift is right in front of you. The chair we were supposed to get on had room for four people.

See? That's no chair. That's a couch!

I had Dad on one side and Mom on the other. Carlos was on the outside.

When our turn was next, I pushed myself forward. We had to get to a red line in the snow, but the chair lift was coming up behind us fast, and it wasn't stopping.

I pumped my way forward and made it!

Then that old couch came up right behind me. It bumped into me, behind my knees. My slippery snow pants made it hard to sit down. Meanwhile, the chair lifted us up. I was in the air but not really all the way in the seat. I felt like I was going to fall and the chair got higher. . . and higher. . . .

I yelled, "Ahhhhhh!"

Dad grabbed my jacket and pulled me backwards, onto the seat. "You're fine, G.G.," he said. "Got you!"

The lift did a few big swings as we got going. My stomach did a couple of flips, too.

Now that I was all the way back on the seat, the swinging of the chair made me smile.

"I did it!"

"You did," said Mom.

We flew way up the mountain, above everybody. I could see people on skis and people on snowboards. I saw lots of runs down the mountain. That's what they call trails that people ski or snowboard down. Kind of silly since NO ONE is running, right?

Ski mountains are strange places, and that's all I have to say about that.

But those runs looked fun. I was getting so excited. Then Carlos had to make fart noises by blowing on his glove. Soooo NOT funny.

Dad said, "Okay, get ready."

And then I saw it. Right in front of us was a sign: "Unload Here."

You know what that means? That means TROUBLE. That means you have to get off. And do you know what's harder than getting on that big flying couch?

You guessed it.

"Time to get off," said Mom.

At the end of the chair lift ride up the hill,
you have to get off. I was NOT excited about that part.

Chapter 11

"Lift up the front of your board," said Dad.

"Keep your balance," said Mom.

"DON'T FALL!" said Carlos.

Well guess what? I didn't fall first. Dad lost his balance and fell toward me. I tried to duck out of the way and ended up on Mom. Then Mom fell sideways. On top of Carlos.

And we all ended up in the snow in one big tangled blob.

The lift stopped. A man came out of a hut and started helping us up. "Everybody okay?"

"I think so," said Dad. He looked at me. "Okay, G.G.?"

Well. I was fine. But I have to say, the lift was not my favorite. I asked, "Does this happen every time?"

Mom laughed. "Sometimes. But it does get easier."

Everybody moved arms and legs and boards. Finally we got untangled. I scooted on my butt and everybody else stood and we got away from that awful couch.

The man went back in the hut and made the lift move again.

"Need help, G.G.?" Dad asked. He pointed to my snowboard.

"Nope!" I was now good at strapping in. I showed him how good.

We did Toad's Road first—totally cool.

Once we were all ready, Dad said, "How about an easy one to start?"

"Toad's Road!" said Carlos.

"Lead the way," said Dad.

First of all, turning on the mountain is A LOT harder than turning on the bunny slope.

And that's all I have to say about that.

Except that by the time we reached the lift again, the only thing I felt good at was the plop and the bounce.

And smash.

And crash.

And THUD.

"Tomorrow will be easier," said Mom.

"The first day is always the hardest," said Dad.

Even Carlos said, "The first day I snowboarded I had bruises EVERYWHERE. Even on my nose."

Ha! Carlos with a purple nose is a funny thought. So I got in line for the lift again, this time just with Dad.

And I didn't even fall getting on. . . or off!

Ha! Almost expert!

When Mom and Carlos got off behind us, Carlos said, "Let's go to the terrain park!"

Mom and Dad had one of those looks. The kind where adults use their eyes to say kids are asking Too Much.

Well. I was ready to shred on the mountain. And, Carlos was being a show off. Which makes me act like a show off right back. It's a problem.

Me and Dad on the flying couch. Yikes!

So even though I was a teeny, tiny, eenie, weenie bit scared, I said, "Yeah! Let's ride some rails!"

"You sure?" asked Dad.

"Yep," I said.

So did I tell you that although I said yes, I was just a teensy bit scared?

No?

True fact.

Chapter 12

Have you ever seen a terrain park? Well it's a wild mess. Big jumps are everywhere. Steep walls and curves are carved into the snow. Plus, there are picnic tables and pipes and all kinds of crazy things that people ski and snowboard on top of.

Say what—snowboard on a table? Grandma Garcia doesn't even let me put my ELBOWS on the table!

But the terrain park is a fun place to be. People do all kinds of weird things. I could watch all day. It was even better than watching a movie (even upside down). Because this was real life.

"Hey, look," said Carlos. He pointed to a guy up the hill, near the biggest jump. "He's going to catch some monster big air."

The guy started slow but then got going really fast. He took off from the jump and did a flip AND a spin. All at the same time!

"Wow," said Carlos. "A rodeo! See that?"

Then a girl started off a smaller jump. But she seemed to change her mind and try to stop. Even I knew this was not going to be good.

"Bail!" yelled Carlos.

The girl hit the snow hard. Her gloves came off, and her scarf got all tangled, but she laughed.

"Ouch," said Carlos. "And look at that bomb hole!"

A flippy twisty thingy off a big jump

is called a rodeo. Cool!

"So where she landed and made that hole in the snow, that's a bomb hole?" I asked.

"Yep," said Carlos. "Hey, there's a little jump right here. Let's go!"

Carlos took off. Since the jump was right in front of him, he wasn't going fast. But when he got to the top, he raised his arms and yelled, "Blast off!"

He flew off the jump, at least a little bit. Then he stopped and yelled back to me, "Come on, G.G."

Well. It wasn't a very big jump. Or very steep.

So kind of slowly, I started toward the jump. I got to the top, raised my arms like Carlos and yelled, "Woo hoo!"

Maybe I was going so slow I didn't even catch some air. But you know what? My stomach did little loops and my legs felt like they were flying and IT WAS SO COOL!

Carlos looked down the slope and said, "Let's go around that corner. That's where the rails are."

Now, I KNOW I said I would ride some rails.

But I thought Carlos should go first.

He took off down the mountain. All I could see was a little bump of snow that led onto a tall, super skinny piece of pipe. How could he possibly ride on that?

I held my breath. He was closer. . . and closer. . . .

And then he went around it! What?

The big rail looked so skinny—scary!

Then I realized, down past the big rail I'd seen, there was a smaller, shorter rail. It was practically on the ground. And Carlos rode over it in kind of a sideways slide.

"Yeah!" he said.

I smiled.

Not only did that look fun, but I could do that!

And so with only one plop along the way, I made it to the rail, rode over it before I could thud or bounce, and I DID IT, TOO!

Okay, true fact. I did bobble and bounce off the end. And that was maybe followed by a little thud.

"Now for the box," said Carlos. He rode just a little further, to something that stuck up like a big box. He rode right over it and off the end.

Okay, now this thing I'd never even heard of. But you know what? I'd fallen so much already today, one more weird new thing seemed like no big deal.

So I pointed my board toward it, slid off the top of the box and—

"Bail!" I yelled as I hit the snow.

That box was so easy to ride and slide right over—it was the easiest thing in the terrain park!

Everybody in my family laughed. We were all so happy to be shredding snowboarders who caught air off jumps, rode the rails and slid off a box at the terrain park.

Finally Dad said, "All right, guys. Time to head down."

"Yeah," said Carlos. "And we can go by the superpipe on the way!"

I asked, "Is that like a halfpipe?"

"Yeah," said Carlos. "It's the *super big* one!"

Uh oh.

Chapter 13

After the terrain park, there was a big hill off to the side. A lot of people stood on top of it.

"That's the top of the superpipe," said Carlos. "Let's go!"

It didn't look too hard. So I followed.

Carlos stopped at a flat spot. I stopped next to him.

Oh.

My.

Gosh.

Down the other side, below us, the snow dropped off like a wall of death.

The superpipe isn't just big—it's GINORMOUS!

The superpipe was carved out of the mountain. It looked like a big, fat snake had slid straight down the slope, digging out a dent in the snow as he went. Except it wasn't like a little dent, it was GINORMOUS. In the middle was a flat part, but on both sides the snow went straight up.

The walls were higher than a volleyball net.

Higher than a basketball hoop.

Higher than the walls of my whole school gym!

Carlos pointed to the top of our wall, where we stood. "This is the deck, where it's flat on top." Then he pointed to the corner, where the wall fell straight down into the pipe. "And that's the lip."

"Duh," I said. I actually didn't know that, but Carlos was showing off. AGAIN.

Of course, Carlos stuck out his tongue. Ugh.

Dad came up next to me and looked down into the superpipe. "Whoa," he said.

"It's crazy, right?" asked Mom, who had come up behind him.

We watched as people snowboarded into the superpipe. Mainly they went up the walls fast, but some did cool twisty things.

An older girl came up next to me. She said, "Hey, little grom. You going?"

I shook my head. I was NOT going anywhere. And that's all I have to say about that!

"Okay," she said. "I'm dropping in."

And then she rode right over the wall of death and into the superpipe. She went up the other wall and flew high into the sky.

"Smooth," said Carlos. "She's going huge!"

As she went down, she rode fast through the flat bottom and then up the other side. . . and then she did a flip.

A FLIP!

Flip + Superpipe = Hero

"Sick," said Carlos. "A McTwist!"

As she went down the superpipe, she did one crazy trick after another. Carlos kept calling her tricks funny names, like "cab three-sixty" and "alley-oop." By the time she got to the bottom of the superpipe, she'd done about six different tricks.

Everybody watching was hooting and yelling and clapping and going crazy!

That girl was my hero.

"Okay, guys," said Dad. "Time to head back."

NO!

I wanted to watch this some more. This was the most fun thing I had seen... *ever*.

"Come on, little grom," said Mom. "We can come back tomorrow."

"What's a grom?"

Dad laughed. "A kid like you who loves to snowboard."

Ha!

We went down, but NOT in the superpipe. We went back to the trail. On the way, I saw that girl again. She was sitting in the snow, watching people go off a jump.

She waved. "Catch you later!"

That night at dinner, Carlos told everybody about the superpipe.

Bell said, "Remember in the car, G.G.? You said 'Halfpipe or nothing!' So are you going on the superpipe tomorrow, G.G.?"

Little sisters are sometimes a really, really, really big pain.

And that's ALL I have to say about THAT.

Chapter 14

For one thing, my family was right: the first day was the hardest. For the next two days, we rode all over the mountain. I jumped any little bump I could find. I took the rails any time I saw one. AND I even started going so fast Dad kept yelling, "Wait for me!"

It was the most fun I've ever had in my whole life. True fact.

For another thing, sometimes I say too much. It's a problem.

So even though every day was the best day *ever*, every night Bell asked if I'd gone down the superpipe yet.

Did I tell you about little sisters?

A PAIN!

So the last day we were at Aunt Christina's and Uncle Frank's, I decided I better do something about that superpipe.

Or I would have to listen to Bell *forever*. Ugh.

Uncle Frank and I went down the trail by the terrain park. First I did that low rail again. Then I watched Uncle Frank do the bigger rail.

Have you ever seen your really old uncle hit the top of a rail, flip sideways and fall in a big mess of flying snow?

Ha! I have, and I can tell you it is super HILARIOUS.

"I caught the nose," said Uncle Frank with a big smile. That's how I knew it was okay to think it was funny and not worry he'd broken all his old bones.

He got up and started riding down the hill. "Let's go check out the superpipe," he said.

I followed, kind of worried.

All right, VERY WORRIED.

When we got to the top of the superpipe, guess who was there?

Yep. . . my new hero, the girl who did the flip.

"Little grom! You dropping in?" she asked.

I decided to tell her my secret. "Well, I told everybody in my family that I'd do the halfpipe. But I'm afraid. I only learned to snowboard this week. And the superpipe is GINORMOUS!"

She nodded. "The superpipe can be pretty gnarly."

"Exactly!" I said.

We both looked down into the superpipe. I had that Oh-My-Gosh moment all over again.

"But you feel like you have to do a halfpipe," said the girl.

"It's a problem," I said.

She nodded. "Follow me."

Well. I kind of didn't want to. But I also kind of did.

So I followed.

Uncle Frank followed me, like the caboose.

We went down the mountain, but not into the superpipe. First we went around it, and then down a run I hadn't been on all week. Near the bottom of the run was a much smaller halfpipe.

Ah ha!

"This is where I started," she said. "It's for beginners and little groms like you."

I was excited. "I could do this one!"

"I bet you can," she said.

"But maybe I could follow you, just for the first time?"

"Let's do it!"

She started into the halfpipe.

And I followed her. Exciting! I was doing it!

The walls made me go fast and I had to turn quick and whoa, it was fun but whoooaaaa I was going backwards!

"Hey, riding fakie already little grom? You rock!"

I did it—I really, really did it! I rode the HALFPIPE!!

Then I was going backwards really fast and it was scary and suddenly I was all wobbly and—

You know what happened next.

Plop.

Bounce!

THUD.

When I got up, the girl was next to me with her hand out for a high five.

"I fell," I said.

She still had her hand out for a high five. "But you did it! That was gutsy."

That means bold.

And brave.

So I gave her a high five. Because you know what? I really and truly rode the halfpipe.

Me getting a high five from a real snowboarder. After I'd done the halfpipe. Awesome!

"I think you even caught some air," she said with a big smile.

How about that?

"You work on this halfpipe for a while," she said, "and then I'll be seeing you over at the superpipe."

"The superpipe?"

"Some day. When you're ready. You'll be dropping in with me."

"You think I could do that?"

"Little grom," she said, "there's no doubt."

And that's what happened when I finally learned to snowboard.

Since spring break was almost over, my family went home that night.

The next day, Isaac and I hung upside down on my couch and I told him all about the magic carpet and the lift and the terrain park and even the halfpipe.

Meanwhile, Isaac had been practicing, so he caught 20 popcorn pieces in a row. So somebody made it to a new record! And I got to learn to shred. Spring break was pretty awesome after all.

And that is all I have to say about that.

Shred on!

THE END

ACKNOWLEDGEMENTS

As always, grateful thanks to the Calabash Broads: Ann Black, Maria Faulconer, Toni Knapp, Susan Rust and Linda DuVal. Their ever-attentive critical eye and expertise is forever invaluable.

Thanks also to the Rocky Mountain Chapter of the Society of Children's Book Writers & Illustrators (SCBWI) for constant professional resources and encouragement. Especially appreciated are the southern Colorado SCBWI gang who bring advice, support and (not least of all) delicious treats to our schmoozes.

To the Panera Indie Pub Group, masters of the online universe, thanks for wisdom, knowledge, infinite support and great lunch chat. Indebtedness goes to DeAnna Knippling, Annie MacFarlane, Cindi Madsen, Jennie Marts, Michelle Major, Chris Myers, Lana Williams and Robin Nolet.

To my family both immediate and extended, you're what it's all about. I'm thankful you're there.

And finally, I'm grateful for the chance to work with Alisa, who brought it all: unwavering enthusiasm, original perspective, general coolness and mad skill. This was probably not the best year to take on such a complicated journey, but we got it done, sister—woo hoo!

~M.M.B.

Thank you to Matt for selling me my first snowboard, the Barfoot Halfpipe 161—it was *way* too big, but it taught me how to ride. To David, for being my best good snowboard buddy all along. To Michael, Travis, Teddy, Ryan and Eli for letting me be one of the dudes, which helped me become the lady I am.

To my coaches, del Giudice, Van Aken and Keene, and trainers Kyle, Clay and Ned—thank you for teaching me sport and encouraging what was good in me. To my teammates, especially Kelly, Gretchen and Tricia—there is something about those days that will always define who I am.

To my girl crew: Jenna, Jonnel, Megan, Susie, Jackie, Deb, Amanda, Julie, Tara, Rachael, Adrienne. . . Thank you for the laughs and for showing me that it was OK to "ride like a girl."

I could never say thank you enough to Kenn Bisio— what an honor to be your mushroom. And many thanks to my fellow mushrooms and Iris family—Rachael, Cora, Leah, Johanna, Heather and Simona. Jenn, you are in a world of your own—an enigma, a beautiful, shining star. I don't think you'll ever know how much I admire you. Also a big thank you to Barry Gutierrez and Larry Price, who took time from their important careers to shape the lives of students.

To my ESPN family—I've learned so much from you and have memories for a lifetime. Particularly to my Research team—DTR!

Jessie Lu, my sister from another mister—you continually encourage me, guide me and remind me to look towards the sunshine.

And my family. My dad and Steph, who spent hours ignoring cold feet to cheer me on in that big, scary superpipe. My sister, Nessie, who defines greatness despite adversity. My mother, who taught me strength despite gender. My grandmother, whose spirit of adventure drives me every day. My grandfather, who taught me pure goodness, and who I miss each and every day. And to my extremely large Italian & Irish family, each and every one who I hold dear to my heart—I love you all.

A huge thank you to my aunt Marty—you have inspired me since I first smelled the chemicals and saw the fresh prints hanging in your Colorado Springs dark room in the early '80s. I have never wanted to be anything more than what you are.

Lastly, but most importantly, to my rocks—husband Paul and minis Sage and Stella. You define me, inspire me, make what I do possible and just straight up make me feel warm and cozy. Love you so much.

~A.M.H.

95

About the Writer and Photographer

Writer **Marty Mokler Banks** has skied since she was a kid but leaves the shredding to her son. She is the author of the popular chapter book *The Adventures of Tempest & Serena*. Her children's picture book, *The Splatters Learn Some Manners,* was a 2010 Colorado Book Award nominee for Children's Literature. A longtime member of the Society of Children's Book Writers & Illustrators (SCBWI), Banks lives in Colorado with her family and dogs. Find her online at MartyMoklerBanks.com or at her blog, ChapterBookChat.wordpress.com.

Photographer **Alisa Mokler Harper** is a former member of the U.S. Snowboard Team and was a two-time competitor at ESPN's X Games. She still shreds any chance she gets, but lately spends more time passing the passion on to her own G.G.s, Sage and Stella. Having moved to the other side of operations, Harper now works in television production for ESPN. She frequently shows her photographs in galleries, online and in sports publications. She lives in Colorado with her family of humans, cats, dogs and horses.

G.G. Snowboards is the first collaboration of the aunt/ niece team of Banks & Harper.

Made in the USA
Middletown, DE
09 October 2015